LOVING THE WRONG MAN 3

MIA BLACK

CHAPTER 1

W e stared at each other for a moment, and then I turned and looked straight ahead through the windshield. Alisha and three of the men were standing in front of the van I was sitting in. They were talking heatedly, then walked towards the back of the car. I turned back towards Que and inched towards the still-open door. I was going to make a run for it. Que noticed what I was doing and shook his head no. Just as I was about to leap out of the van, Andre jumped into the seat next to Que and slammed the door. The other two men entered my van and sat behind me. Alisha sat down in the front passenger seat and turned her head to face me.

"The fun is just beginning," she said, and winked at me.

I was pushed forward. My arms were pulled roughly behind me and zip tied, and I felt a cloth bag go over my head, leaving me in complete darkness. Over the course of the drive, no one spoke or even played music. I didn't know where they were taking me, or if they were separating me from Que. All I felt were the subtle bumps and turns of the road. After what seemed like hours of driving, the car came to a halt, and the doors were opened and then slammed shut again. I felt the desert heat as my door was opened and I was roughly pulled out of the car. The narrow barrel of a gun was pressed into my back.

"Move!" the masculine voice behind me commanded and I was on my way. I walked down a straight, narrow path. I didn't want to make any sudden movements that might cause one of them to shoot me. Shortly after, my foot hit a solid block and I almost tripped. If I fell, I wouldn't be able to break my fall.

"Steps. Three of them," the voice said. I lifted up my legs and walked up the stairs, then felt two arms push me through the door and down onto a couch. The bag was removed from my head. It took a moment for my eyes to adjust before I realized I was sitting in a living room. I looked over to my left and saw Que sitting there, staring straight ahead. His eyes were still black and the blood from his nose had crusted over on his lip. They didn't even bother to clean him up. To keep myself from crying, I turned my head away to stare at the wall.

We were in the living room of an ordinary one-story residential home. Although the curtains were drawn, I could see between the small crack and recognized the desert mountains in the background. We were still in Arizona. Alisha walked into the room shortly after and picked up a chair. She sat down right in front of Que. I saw his jaw set out of the corner of my eye as he stared through her.

"Does this place look familiar, babe?" Alisha asked him.

Que continued to stare at the wall.

"You're so very good at this. The armor, the resolve. So sexy," Alisha cooed as she leaned over, her lips almost touching Que's. He continued to stare straight ahead.

In a condescending tone, she continued,

"Now, I know you told us not to hit that lick, but it was oh so tempting."

Que continued to stare straight ahead. Alisha cocked her head to the side.

"I gotta keep you pretty." She smiled. Licking her thumb, she wiped away the dried blood that caked on Que's lip. "And although you did tell us not to take the mission, we were still going to split the money with you. That's what loyalty is about. Taking care of each other, even when one backs out. So imagine my surprise and utter heartbreak when you left me for dead."

Alisha got out of the chair and then stepped away for a second. She stared at the wall with her hand to her mouth. She then suddenly turned around and slapped Que across the face. His head rocked back. I wanted to kill her. He quickly composed himself continued to stare at the wall behind Alisha.

"For fucking dead, Evan. Andre called you to come and get us, and you left me for dead." She screamed and lifted up her shirt. Near her right rib, underneath her breast, was patch of discolored rubbery skin, the remnants of a bullet wound. I took a deep breath.

"You're going to make this right, Evan." Alisha said, composing herself. "And there's only one way you can do it. Scottsdale. Fashion. Square. Set it up."

Que looked at her in shock. "The fuck you mean Scottsdale Fashion Square? I told you I ain't about that life no more. I ain't doing shit!" Que yelled.

Alisha walked over to me. "I had a feeling you'd say that." She grabbed my hair and pulled my head back. "I will make you watch. Andre, shall we?" Alisha forced my mouth open and Andre walked up to me, smiling. I watched him unbuckle his pants. I closed my eyes and tried to move my head away. She held me in a vice grip. Fearing the inevitable, I started to dissociate. I began to imagine myself on the beach in the south of France with Que. As we lazed about in the sand, he grabbed my hand and kissed it. I smiled at him.

In the distance of my mind, I heard Que stand up and the cock of a gun as it was taken off its safety. I heard Alisha say calmly, "And after he finishes throat fucking her, I'm going to make you watch me kill her. The choice is really yours." Her voice was then replaced with the sounds of the ocean.

I felt Que's eyes on me. As warm as the sun. "Fuck it. Fine. Let's do this," he said, defeated.

"That's more like it." Alisha replied.

CHAPTER 2

I opened up my eyes and stared at Que. Alisha walked into the kitchen as Andre buckled his belt. He walked over to Que and patted him on the shoulder before turning to me.

"Never thought I'd see the day you'd get soft over a bitch. She cute though. Glad to have you back on the team," Andre said as he walked into the kitchen. I forced my mind to return to the real world. I had to stay alert. Slowly opening my eyes, I noticed that besides the five men and Alisha, there were at least four other men in the room. It was a large living room, but sparsely furnished, with two end tables and one other couch. The other men sat around in foldable chairs. They all laid in wait for Que, as if they would take flight if he made even the smallest move.

One of them, a slender light skinned man with a long braid, stood over Que. Que looked up.

"Tito!" Que said.

Tito looked at him. "You were like a brother to me. To all of us, and you left us in the cold, bruh."

Que refused to look at him. He stared at the wall and rubbed his hands together. "I told you not to go. I told all of you that. I tried to protect you, fam, and I would've got you out, but you still rolled with her." Que then looked back up to him.

"Once I got in, that's all I could do. You saw how she was with your girl. It's life or death man. No in between," Tito said.

Que nodded his head as Tito walked away from him. I looked around the room and noticed that the men were still staring at him. Que looked around at all of them and smirked. It seemed like they wanted to say something to him but couldn't really find the words. I could tell they still considered him their leader.

"The youngest are usually the bravest. Anyone else have anything to say to me, while I'm here? Because you heard Alisha. We got shit to do," Que commanded.

I looked around again. No one said anything. Que then leaned back into the couch. However, there was one man in particular who stared at Que with such hate. If looks could kill... He looked to be about 6'1" with brown skin. He had a low-cut fade with round dark brown eyes. A deep scar ran from his temple to his cheek. He gave me the once over and winked at me. I looked away.

"I don't know why y'all niggas saluting him like he still running the show. That nigga left us. Alisha acting like she need this nigga to hit this mission. Now that he got this bitch here, he gonna run off like he did the last time."

He then turned to Que and stood up. He slowly walked over to the couch. Que looked over at him and smirked. He stood over him. "I would've put two hot ones in this nigga's head off rip."

"Streetz, my nigga," Que responded sarcastically.

"Don't Streetz, my nigga me. Motherfucker,

you a real cold nigga. No motherfucking loyalty. After all the shit we did for you, you were gonna let us rot in there and keep all the money. Luckily Alisha was able to get me and a couple of the other niggas outta the bing, but we still got fam in there."

"I knew I didn't recognize any of these niggas," Que interrupted.

Streetz continued. "How can you do that to the only mothafuckas who had your back? Who took you in, when you had no family?"

Que shook his head and looked up at Streetz. He stood up. "There was eleven of us and we each coulda had a cool five mil between us. But when that greedy bitch decided that wasn't enough, y'all followed. I told you niggas where to put your money and how to set shit up but you didn't listen, so…"

Streetz's anger flared. "You knew we needed to hit that last lick to keep shit straight for everyone. If you had've been there, shit wouldn't have went down the way it did. But you didn't show up and Alisha had to handle the situation, much like she did with getting me, Andre and--"

Que stood up and interrupted him. "Shit would've went left regardless. I told you not to do it. I told you it would be too big a job to pull. Art Basel. Seriously, come the fuck on. I know motherfuckas love to dream big, but got damn, have some sense about your shit. And besides, fuck all this loyalty shit. Niggas was getting stupid, plotting and planning, trying to take the reins from me. I had a bunch of you niggas try me over the years, but when you put Alisha up to it, I knew it was my time to get out and change shit around. And that included letting you niggas fall. You was the ones not showing no loyalty. Not me."

Streetz squared his shoulders and stepped towards Que with his hands balled into a fist. Que looked down and smiled. Out of the corner of my eye, I noticed a bigger man stand up and reach behind his pocket. I was silently praying that Que would shut up and sit down.

"So am I sorry you got fucked in prison, pretty boy? Not quite. But then again, I used to always wonder about you." Que then nodded his head to the right. "Diamonds are girl's best friend, not mine."

The man took out his gun and ran towards Que. He cocked the gun and put it towards Que's head. The other two followed suit. Que just stood there and continued to stare at Streetz. I closed my eyes again, waiting for the blast.

"Blow my brains out and there goes the plans," Que continued.

Alisha and Andre ran out of the kitchen. "What the fuck is going on here? Stand the fuck down."

Streetz turned to Alisha. "But he was talking shit."

Alisha walked up to Streetz and pulled him away. She took his face into her hands and leaned his head against hers. "Let him talk shit. It's all he can do. You're the one that has the real heart," she said soothingly.

Alisha turned to the men who still had their guns drawn on Que. "I said, stand down." She commanded. The men lowered their guns. "Too much testosterone. I can't leave you boys alone for three minutes without there being some kind of problem. This is why I hate family reunions." She fluffed her hair and sat down. "Come on Que, take a seat. We got a lot of planning to do. As I was saying before, we are going to run a mission at the Scottsdale Fashion Square."

Que smirked at Streetz and sat down. He

glanced at me. "Why that mall of all malls? Isn't that too small time for you?"

Alisha turned to him and smiled. "That is why I want to do it. Smaller city but still with plenty of legit shit. Bulgari, Tiffany, David Yurman." She then looked at me, and then at my wrist. "Cartier." She then turned back to Que.

"I already got the floor plans and the stocking schedule for each store. They alternate stocking between Tuesdays and Thursdays. Different merchandise for different days. Tuesdays are metals, Thursdays are gems."

Que looked at me and then back at Alisha. "Can she leave the room? I don't want her hearing about any of this. She ain't a part of it."

Alisha looked at me and smiled, "What else do you have to hide, Evan? She is a part of this. You made her a part of this. She should really know who she is dealing with." She winked at me. I turned my head to the wall. "I need her to have some stake in this, besides fucking you."

Que glanced at me, and then faced Alisha.

Alisha continued. "Loose gems where they can set and design them on site. The times for restocking is from one to five in the morning.

Normally, this mall is heavily guarded except for four hours out of the day. Five-thirty to nine-thirty, right before the mall opens. They have a very complex security system. As we all know, malls in more affluent areas have more cameras because of car thieves. However, lucky for us, we ain't going for cars. The square has five cameras per 30 square feet. They use a combination of CCTV cameras and small domed cameras, some of them recessed, which would normally mean that we wouldn't be able to document the camera movements."

Que nodded his head, "Exactly!"

Alisha winked at Que again and continued. "However, luckily for us, the monitors reset the recordings between the hours of 5:30 and 9:30AM to clear up the server for the following business day. During this time, we can redirect the server to provide the previous day's footage.

Que shook his head. "You niggas must love jail. You don't learn. This heist, like the last one, will fail from the beginning. How will you shut down a complicated system? Five cameras per 30 square feet. You don't think all of those cameras are on one server? You don't actually think that there is only one server? There could be a minimum one or three for all we know. The resources aren't there. Where is the money? Where are the computers?" He looked around at the men sitting around the living room. He avoided my stare. He seemed to be embarrassed that I was witnessing him in his natural element. I'll admit though, it was a little bit of a turn on. I was watching him take charge. I bit my lower lip.

He continued. "It's too complicated for what we have and you still haven't designated who will do what? Who will be the hackers? Who will be the security guards? Who will be the lookout, all that shit? "

Alisha rolled her eyes and looked at Andrc. She smiled warmly. "We learned from the last time. Right baby?"

Andre looked at Que menacingly and nodded.

"We will do this tomorrow night. We ready."

I sat there dumbfounded. I couldn't believe what I was hearing. They were going to rob the Scottsdale Fashion Square and I was privy to all of the information. I officially felt like I lost everything. At the very least, if they got away with this, they might kill me because I knew too much. If they were caught, I would automatically go to jail. Even though I came from money, I'm still black, and they could very well throw me in jail as an accomplice. I was a carrot for Que to take on the heist. She banked on him doing anything to keep me safe, and she might hurt me just to get back at him, whether he complied or not. Either way, things would never be the same.

"I'm a little hungry. Let's go over plans after we eat, shall we?" Alisha stood up and walked up to Que. "Welcome back to the team baby. We missed you."

Andre and Streetz left to get food for everyone. They returned with pizza and soda. They didn't offer any food to me or Que. I could care less, because I knew that if I ate any thing, I would've thrown it up. They kept us on the couch for most of the day. During that time, I watched them bring out large maps and unwrap them. I tried to drown out what they did by closing my eyes and daydreaming. Although I was so tired, I was afraid to fully sleep. I didn't want to run the risk of being raped.

At nightfall, Alisha came over and lifted me up out of the seat. "I'm mean, but I'm not heartless. Since we are the only two ladies in here, I think I should give you some privacy."

I looked at her in fear as she led me down the hallway and into the bathroom. "I know you have to pee. Go head."

I turned around and showed her my zip tied arms. "I can't." I said weakly.

She looked down. "Gotcha." She reached in her back pocket and took out her switchblade. She reached down and cut the zip ties away from my hand. She made sure to draw a little bit of blood from my wrist. It hurt but I refused to flinch. She took both hands and turned me around.

"If you think I'm going to let you go around free hand, you got me fucked up on that one too." She reached into her pocket again and took out another set of zip ties. She tied my hands together again, but at least I was able to unbutton and pull down my pants. I walked into the bathroom and she shut the door behind me.

I pulled down my pants and sat on the toilet. I just sat there for a few minutes and began to cry. I was unable to go to the bathroom. The little bit of water I drank sprang from my eyes. Alisha knocked softly on the door.

"Shit or get off the pot. You have a few minutes. I'm not going to stand here all night."

"Okay." I whimpered. I was able to squeeze out a few drops. I cleaned myself up and washed my hands. Alisha opened up the door and pulled me out. She took me by the elbow and continued to lead me down the hallway, where she opened up another door. Inside the room was one single bed.

"Don't worry." Alisha whispered to me. "I won't let anyone do anything to you, even if Evan decides to get out of line, which I don't think he will. You proved to be quite valuable."

She pushed me into the bedroom and shut the door. I sat there looking around to see if I could possibly escape. Although having my hands tied in front of me was way more comfortable than the roughly ten hours of damn near sitting on my hands, my movements were still limited. I was also afraid of what would happen if I got caught. I sat down on the bed and laid down. The tears began to flow again and I cried myself to sleep.

I woke up to someone caressing my face in the dark. I was about to scream when a hand covered my mouth. I panicked and tried to thrash, but he leaned against my body, keeping me from moving and being able to defend myself. I knew not to trust her, or anyone. I let my mind wander, imagining myself in the Virgin Island, swimming in the Atlantic Ocean. I felt my body float on top of the water, the rise and ebb of the waves. The heat of his body on top of mine became the tropical heat. Lips close to my ear, a familiar voice whispered "Jazzy, I am so sorry about putting you in harm's way." I began to relax and returned to the dark room. Through the darkness, I recognized Que.

"I thought I did all of what I could do to protect you and I failed you. But I promise you that you will be safe no matter what happens. You will walk out of the this with no problems."

I missed his scent and the way he felt. He continued, "Nod your head if you heard me, baby. I know I startled you by the way I came in here, but I didn't want them to know I snuck away to see you."

My body continued to relax under his. I nodded my head in response. He kissed my forehead, the tip of my nose and then finished with a gentle peck on my lips. "Even though you will survive this, I might not. Those niggas out there want my blood, and even if everything goes off without a hitch, they may still kill me for walking out on them. If something happens to me, just know that I love you. I loved you since I first saw you."

My heart broke at that point. All I did was deny my heart to him, and made him jump through hoops. I admit it. I loved him since day one and it took this moment for us to speak it into the world. I nodded my head as the tears flowed. He slowly kissed them away.

"I love you too." I whispered.

Que kissed my forehead again. He then got up quickly and left the room. I laid there in the stillness of the room, surrounded by nothing but darkness and my tears.

I awoke to Alisha ripping open the curtains in the bedroom. "Wake up sunshine."

I turned my head towards Alisha. "You need to take a shower. Sorry you don't have a change of clothes, but at least you'll be clean."

I sat up on the bed. "How am I going to bathe myself?"

She turned around and gave me a once over. "I know a few who would love to help you with that. I'll stay in the bathroom until you're done."

I nodded my head, "Okay."

She helped me up and led me towards the door. "By the way, how's that cut on your arm?"

I turned my head and narrowed my eyes at her. With a slight smirk, I answered unbothered, "What cut?"

Alisha led me to the bathroom and cut the zip ties from my arms. She handed me a wash-cloth and a bar of soap. "No lotion, doll face."

I turned on the water and got undressed. I wrapped my hair into a bun and stepped into the shower. The hot water felt amazing against my skin.

"You have five minutes." Alisha said through the curtain. I quickly bathed and turned off the faucet. Alisha opened up the shower curtain and handed me a towel. "I see why Quinton is head over heels. You thicker than a snicker."

I quickly took the towel and wrapped it around me. She smiled and turned her back to me. I leaned over and picked up my clothes. After a few minutes, Alisha asked me, "Are you finished?"

"Yes." I replied. She then turned around

and zip tied my hands again. I was led back to the living room, where the men were looking at laptops. I looked for Que and I couldn't find him. My heart started to race. I tried to remain calm as I sat down. A few minutes later, Que walked in, cleaned up and carrying a bag. He smiled at me and reached into the bag. Handing me an apple, he said to me, gently, "Eat."

I smiled and took the apple from him. When he noticed my zip tied hands, his jaw set and he turned to Alisha. "You stay with the damn zip ties. What she gonna do?"

Alisha turned to him. "Your little spitfire tried to attack me yesterday. Unless you check your chick, I'm gonna keep old girl tied up until she learns to keep her hands to herself."

Que turned to me and smiled. Winking at me, he said, "She'll be fine." Que walked into the kitchen and returned with a pair of scissors. I lifted up my hands and he cut the ties. I ate the apple.

I was barely able to keep the little bit of food and water that I was able to consume down. My stomach was in knots and my body ached from sleeping on my side the whole night.

"She shouldn't be around when we really

start talking about shit. How do we know she won't call the police?" Streetz asked.

"I been saying that." Que said sarcastically. "But you niggas don't listen."

"I wanted her to know just enough to think twice before saying anything to the cops. But you're right. Andre, take her to the back room."

Andre smiled and stepped forward. "Ain't nothing but a word."

Que's eyes narrowed and his jaw tightened in anger. "I got this." Que picked me up off the couch and gently led me to the back bedroom. He turned me around and kissed me.

"Stay vigilant." He said and closed the door behind him.

The rooms were unevenly cooled. Whereas I was damn near shivering in the living room, the bedroom was sweltering. I didn't want to lay in the bed, which was completely bathed in sunlight, so to keep cool and to be able to listen in, I leaned against the door and sat down. I was able to hear everything.

Alisha's voice rang out. "Okay boys, listen up. It's almost show time. Andre, you got the security uniforms. You and Tito will monitor Cartier. Donis and June, you two have Tiffany.

Sticks and Jay, you got David Yurman. Evan, you will be disarming the security system and servers. Streetz, you're getaway. Me and Tall got Bulgari. So just to go over this one more time. We all work in unison. At exactly 5:35AM, we strike and go for the most bang for the buck. We have 25 minutes to make some magic and will reconvene at the loading dock at exactly 6:00AM. To put some fire under your belly, if you not there, you will get left behind. We all ride together except for Evan. He needs to be able to create a proxy and disarm the server. Evan, did you check the software?"

"It's all good." Que replied.

"This will be our last rendezvous, boys. Let's make this one count. It's good to see the team back together."

I was suddenly overcome with exhaustion and I crawled over to the bed. I completely blacked out.

In the middle of the night, I heard shuffling outside of the door. "She shouldn't come with us." I heard Que say.

"I'm not gonna leave her here. She might run." Alisha replied.

"She won't run. I know she won't."

"How you know?" Alisha asked.

"Because… she loves me." Que replied softly.

"They always do. So did I. But unlike us, you love her too. That's what makes this so much better for me. This means you won't fuck shit up so quickly. I got your kryptonite, Superman. She comes with us, but she rides with me."

I closed my eyes quickly as Que opened the door. He walked over to the bed and shook me awake.

"Jazzy, wake up." I sat up in the bed and focused my eyes on Alisha who was standing in the doorway. I got up and walked out of the room. As we walked out of the living room and into the cool night air, I turned around to watch Que grab his computer bag and get into his car. I went to follow him. Alisha said as she grabbed my arm and led me to the van.

"Not so fast, thickness. You rollin' with me." I was thrown into the back seat and we drove off.

We turned a few blocks and parked the car. Alisha, Andre and I got out of the car and walked towards a security vehicle. Streetz was behind the wheel. I was pushed into the back of the van with the six other men. Alisha got into the front seat next to Streetz. Andre sat next to me and ran his hand up my thigh and tried to touch my sugar spot. I tried my best to stay completely still. Alisha turned her head towards the back.

"I know there's a pretty young thing back there, boys. And it's been a few days since you've had some trim, but no matter how tempting it is, don't touch her."

Andre removed his hand from my thigh. We drove off.

CHAPTER 3

You could move in secrecy on the streets of Phoenix. Although most areas were beautiful and well-kept, the neighborhoods were not well-lit. The security van moved unnoticed and in silence. No one spoke inside. After what seemed like an hour, we finally arrived at the Scottsdale Fashion Square. It looked much different at night. It looked huge, scary and abandoned. No one could hear you scream if something happened. They drove up to the loading dock with Que pulling up right beside them. Andre opened the back door and stepped outside. Out of the corner of my eye, I saw Alisha looking at her watch. Andre walked to the front of the loading dock, lifted up the door, and waited. The rest of the men exited out of the back of the van and closed the door behind them. Each one walked up the ramp.

Streetz looked to his left and nodded his head. Alisha also got out of the car and walked up the ramp. She looked towards the left of the van and nodded her head. The door opened and Que got into the car, holding his computer. Streetz watched as Que typed on the computer. He nodded his head, and Que nodded back.

"In five minutes, everything will be set and they can go in. After that, you know what to do," Que said. Streetz nodded. Que opened up the door again and got out of the car. He walked up the ramp. I still couldn't believe that he was doing this, or how calm he was about all of this. I wondered how we would get away with this. Que walked up to Alisha and said a couple of words to her. She looked back towards the car at Streetz, then back at Que, and nodded her head. She pulled out a gun and handed it to Que, who took it and hugged her. I felt a little pang of jealousy in my heart. Que then turned around and walked back down the ramp, turning toward the left. The doors finally opened to the back of the mall, and Alisha and the rest of the men walked inside.

I sat there. Streetz turned around and faced me. We locked eyes for a moment. I watched his jaw tighten. After what seemed like forever, we heard the sound of the alarms. I panicked. Streetz turned around.

"Shit, too soon E. Get her out of the car. NOW!" Streetz screamed.

He struggled to open the door. I didn't know where to go or what to do. I moved towards the back door of the van. Que opened the back door to the van and pulled me out of the car. I heard gunshots as Que opened the door to his car and pushed me inside. Streetz looked over at Que and rolled down the window.

"I'll divert this shit. Meet me at the rendezvous point!" Streetz screamed before starting the car and backing up. Andre came out, shooting. Que nodded. I ducked as Quinton got into the driver's side and turned on the car.

"Hold on!" He yelled as he put the car in gear and stomped on the gas pedal. Turning his head around, he sped in reverse out of the driveway. Once we were at the end of the alley, he put the car in drive, swerved the car around and we took off. We sped down Scottsdale Road as we saw the blue and red lights in the distance. He slowed up the car, to watch where the police were going. They were all heading towards the mall. We looked to be in the clear for the moment. As we hit the red light, I noticed a large car coming up behind us in the distance. Streetz was right behind us, following us on Scottsdale Road. We saw a few more police flashers behind the security van. Streetz then pulled up in front of our car and drove past us. He made a hard right at the next stop sign. We saw the police cars fly past us. Que stayed at the stop sign until the last police car disappeared around the corner. We made a right onto a residential neighborhood.

We drove a few more miles until we came upon the entrance to a large apartment complex. Que made another hard right and tried to find a parking space to hide out.

"Stay here until I tell you to get out."

"Why are we here?" I asked.

"Rendezvous point."

We slouched down in the seat.

"I want to make sure the cops are cool

before we do anything else. They looking to stop anyone they see out. Plus, the sun is coming up, so it will be a little bit better for us to maneuver. They didn't catch our faces. We're gonna have to…"

Que got quiet as he looked in the rear view mirror. I turned around and looked out the back window. We saw another white van pull up and park next to us.

Que looked at me. "Quick, Jazzy, get out of the car." Que flung the door open and ran to my side of the car. He opened up my door and pulled me out. "Follow me." Holding my hand, we ran through the neighborhood. We saw a small break between the apartments and ran down the small pathway which led to the back alley. We opened up the gate and ran through.

"I can't keep going, Que." I said.

"We are almost there. I'm going to find somewhere for us to rest. I promise. Just a little but farther."

We continued to run down the alley until we ran into a brick wall.

"Fuck! Fuck! Fuck! Fuck! Wrong place. Wrong fucking place. Damn, where's Streetz?" Que said and hit the wall. I looked at him.

"Streetz? He was about to kill you. You trust him?"

He looked around as he spoke to me. "That's my boy. He went down with the rest of them, but he the only one who understood what I was trying to do and how I was betrayed. I kept money on his books. We had to do that shit so Alisha and the rest of them niggas wouldn't suspect anything." He rounded the small corner and saw a narrow opening. "Come this way."

With tears streaming down my face, I said to him, "Que, I can't. Please." With only surviving on a few cups of water, one apple and adrenaline, my body finally succumbed. Que caught me as I fell to the ground. He swooped me up and cradled me in his arms.

"Okay, babe." He said, kissing my forehead. "We can sit for a few minutes. We're safe here for the moment."

We heard footsteps coming towards us. We looked up and there was Streetz running towards us. "Fuck, man! Houdini ass nigga, how the fuck you get away from the cops?"

"Black magic my nigga." Streetz said. He slowed up as he approached us.

"How the fuck I got the wrong place?" Que asked.

"You would've got caught up if you went to the original spot. It's all good, this is the other side of the complex. We can still reach the car if we go through that narrow passageway. The car is waiting."

"Is it in the same spot?" Que asked.

"Ready and waiting."

Que helped me up. Just as he was about to push me into the narrow walkway, we heard the sound of guns cocking. We froze. It was all over. They found us and were going to kill us.

"Turn around." Lights flashed on Streetz, Que and I. We turned around. It was the police. "Put your hands up." We saw the flash of metal as the two police officers pointed their guns at us. All three of us put our hands in the air.

"Now slowly back up until your back hits the wall." We did as we were told. "Now turn around slowly and place your hand on the wall," the police officer said as he walked up towards us with his gun still drawn. We turned around slowly. Que looked at me. We all placed our hands on the brick wall. The two police officers

patted Que and Streetz down and then handcuffed them.

"We need back up for three perps, two
males and one female. They may be connected
with the attempted robbery of the Scottsdale
Fashion Square. Our location is the north
alleyway of the Stonegate Apartments between
Sarensen and Arroyo Road."

"Turn around slowly, ma'am with your arms
up. You can sit down." I watched as the first cop
escorted Streetz and then Que to their car. A
few moments later, another cop car drove up,
lights flashing. I was then searched by a female
cop and handcuffed. I heard the dreaded words
that I hoped would never be applied to me.

In a monotone, the female officer said, "You
have the right to remain silent. Anything you say
can and will be used against you in the court of
law. You have the right to an attorney present
before any questioning. If you can't afford an
attorney, one will be appointed to represent you
before any questioning. Do you understand
these rights?

Choking back tears, I nodded weakly and
said, "Yes."

She nodded her head and led me to her car.

They took us to the police station and we were separated. They took my name and information. They then took me for my mugshot. I didn't have much property for them to seize. I allowed them to take my necklace and love bracelet. I was fingerprinted and a full body search was conducted on me. I fought back tears as I was touched in places that Que hadn't even felt. I was fingerprinted and placed in holding while they searched my name for any warrants. The holding cell was full of prostitutes. I sat in the corner, glad that I got over my reluctance in giving the police my jewelry. I could sometimes rock with the best of them, but I don't think I could have taken on these four rough looking females.

I must have been in holding for a few hours when a female officer walked up and called out my name.

"Jazmine Turay."

"Yes." I replied.

"You're free to go."

I stood up and walked out of the holding cell. She led me to the main desk and gave me my release papers. She continued, "You're lucky. Both of the males you were with said that you had nothing to do with anything. We also ran your records and you don't have any warrants. Here are your papers." She handed them to me. "Property pick up is located in Room 204. Go up the stairs and make a left. It will be the second door on the right.

"Thank you."

I walked up the stairs and entered the waiting room. There were four people ahead of me. I gave them my paperwork and after about ten minutes they came back with a plastic bag containing my two items. As I put them on, the police officer asked me, "How were you able to afford these items? Love bracelets aren't cheap."

I smiled. "Considering the circumstances, I will answer. My mother is a doctor and my father is a lawyer. I also have my own business as a freelance graphic designer with customers in New York as well as here."

The police officer shook his head. "How do you types get caught up with them?"

"I'm not caught up with them." I responded.

"Let's hope it stays that way."

CHAPTER 4

I t must've been early afternoon by the time I was released. As I walked out of the police station, I was at a complete loss at how I was going to get home. I recognized I was in downtown Phoenix, and knew which streets to take to get back to the hotel. Although I knew how to drive the streets, I didn't know the bus routes and I didn't have my cell phone on me. I knew I would have to ask someone to let me borrow theirs. I walked a few blocks away from the detention center. I didn't want people to know where I came from. I walked up to a young lady standing at the bus stop.

"Hello?"

"Hi," the young lady responded.

"I was wondering if I could call a taxi on your cell phone. Mine's just died and I need to get home," I said.

"Sure." The young woman reached into her purse and handed me the phone.

I used Yelp to dial the taxi company. After a two-minute conversation, my ride would be here in about five minutes. I gave them my location and hung up the phone.

"Thank you," I said to the woman and handed her back her phone.

Sure enough, a few minutes later, a yellow cab showed up. An older Nigerian man, about 45 years old, was my driver.

"Where to?" he asked, in a soft Igbo lilt.

"Royal Palms Hotel and Spa. However, I do need to let you know, that I left my wallet at the hotel, so I will need to go into my room and get it. Can you wait for five minutes?"

"Yes, I can. It will charge you though," He answered.

"That's fine. It's the least I can do for inconveniencing you. Thank you."

I leaned my head back and closed my eyes as we drove in silence. After about twenty minutes, I was dropped off to my hotel. Over the course of the last couple days, it was refreshing to see the familiar faces at the front desk. I was so scared that someone may have been hurt when Alisha and her crew kidnapped me and Que. The exchange was friendly as I asked for a new key card. It was as if nothing happened. I ran to the suite and everything was still in the same place. I got my wallet and took out forty dollars. I ran back to the front of the car and paid the driver and gave him a 20-dollar tip. He thanked me and drove off.

I walked back to my room and sank into the darkness. Despite the 95-degree heat and the air conditioning not being turned on for the last couple days, the room felt dark and strangely cool. Que wasn't here and I was terrified. I only knew what happened to Que and Streetz. No word on Andre or Alisha or anyone. I knew the police arrived on the scene, but did they really capture everyone? They may know where I am was. I never got over how Andre would look at me at times.

I walked over to my phone which, was still on the charger. I saw a notification on the news about Que and his theft ring. I all of a sudden had a terrible headache. The way my eyes hurt,

I knew I wasn't able to read everything. I walked over to the couch and sat down. I leaned over and turned on the TV. I leaned my head back. Something higher must have had me in mind, as the Chew was interrupted by a breaking news report.

I closed my eyes and listened.

"Breaking news. An elaborate break-in was staged at the Scottsdale Fashion Square around 6AM this morning. The ten suspects, including its fugitive ringleader Evan Miles, arrested in the break-in were a part of an infamous Miami-based theft ring. Initially the ring leader was said to be hiding out in New York City. However, it was later found out that Evan Miles was hiding out in Phoenix, Arizona. The suspects were caught before any damage was done. However, the mall will remain closed until all evidence is gathered. We will have more information as the story breaks."

I breathed a sigh of relief. They were all caught, so I could relax a little. But so was my Que. The weight of the events of the last few days finally caught up to me. My headache began to subside as the tears streamed down my face. I collapsed on the couch and fell asleep.

I refused to leave the hotel. After another day or so, I was able to get some of my appetite back. I must have lost around ten pounds over the last three days. I eased myself back into eating, focusing on eating the fruit that we had in the fridge. Even though everyone was in jail, I was still vigilant about my surroundings and would only eat at the hotel restaurant. Some of the staff wondered where Que was. I just explained that he was out visiting family. Other times, I stayed in the suite with the curtains drawn and ordered room service. I had to find ways to normalize myself. Luckily, my Phoenix clients were under-standing and allowed me to work more from home.

After about another three days, I heard the door open. I ran into the kitchen and grabbed a knife.

"Jazzy, it's me," I heard Que say as he closed the door behind him. When I saw him, I grew weak. I put down the knife and ran over to him, hugging him, trying to melt my body into him. He smelled, and his breath stunk as he showered my face with kisses, but he was here and that's all that mattered. I ran his bathwater and prepared his toothbrush, then led him into the bathroom.

"Let me take care of you," I said as I began to undress him. As he lowered himself into the bathtub, I turned on the spa jets and started to rub his back. He leaned his head against the rim of the tub and closed his eyes, rubbing them. I lathered up his body and rinsed him off. Reaching down into the water, I began to massage his manhood with my right hand. I felt him grow hard as he began to move against my hand.

"Just relax honey," I said and nibbled on his ear. A few minutes later I felt his cock harden and jump as he released. I helped him out of the tub and dried him off. He turned to me as I handed him a pair of boxers.

"Can I have a few minutes to myself?" he asked.

I nodded my head and closed the door behind me. I sat near the bathroom door as I heard him on turn on the water, I hung my head and cried.

We went to sleep, entangled in each other's embrace. Later on, I awoke to the smell of garlic and tomato sauce. I walked outside to find

Que in his natural element. As I sat down at the table, Que looked up and smiled at me.

"It will be as normal as possible," he reassured me.

"I know. So what are we having for dinner?" I asked.

"Spaghetti with mozzarella and romano cheese filled meatballs," he answered.

"Sounds amazing," I replied.

Que winked at me. "It will be."

Cooking was his therapy. He would talk to me when it was the right time.

"Go ahead and relax yourself. I got this."

I nodded and walked up to him. I gave him a kiss on the cheek and walked back into the bedroom. I had to calm my stomach down so I could eat. It was still in knots.

An hour later, Que knocked on the door gently and said, "Jazzy, dinner is ready."

I got up and opened the door. Que had set out two plates of spaghetti with two glasses of red wine. It looked and smelled amazing. I sat down in front of my plate. Que sat down next to me and stared at me. I looked at my plate and then back at Que, feeling slightly nauseated.

Que reached up and grabbed my hand. "You can't eat, huh?"

I looked down at his hand and nodded my head.

He continued, "I will start. Hopefully this will ease your mind. You need to eat baby, you losing all that thickness I fell in love with."

I laughed and looked up at him.

"They held me because of prior suspicion. I was able to post bail but I have to appear in court in two weeks. However, there were inconsistencies in the story because although I was the ring leader, I wasn't involved in the last heist that got everyone a record. But in order to make the charges stick, they are basically saying that I sent the team out. That was never my style, as you saw over the last few nights. I involve myself in everything. But because of what Alisha did with naming me and saying that I called the shots off location, I don't know what the outcome of the trial will be."

I busted out crying. Que wiped away my tears and caressed my face.

"Shhh," he said, "It's all the memories. Memories are what matters. That's why I never said anything to you about the old me. I want you to have nothing but positive memories of me. I will make the most of the next two weeks that I have with you. Anything you want, anything you need. It is yours. I am yours. I've always been yours."

"I'm afraid to leave the house." I replied.

"You don't have to be. They're all locked up. I have some people on the inside that'll let me know if anyone is released. The way I set things up, they are all being held without bond."

We sat there in silence.

"I want you to tell me everything. Show me the good and bad. Show me where you grew up, where you went to school. I want to know the real you."

Que swallowed hard and nodded his head. "I'm all yours."

The familiar heat of his body helped ease me into sleep that night. Tucked away in his arms, I finally felt safe.

I woke up in the morning to the smell of blueberry pancakes and sausage. I walked out of the bedroom just as Que was setting the plates on the table. In addition to the pancakes and sausage, he also prepared poached eggs with avocado and a strawberry relish. There was a carafe of fresh orange juice also on the table. I sat down and smiled.

Que sat across from me. "Hello, my name is Evan Aaron Miles. Blueberry pancakes and sausage was my favorite breakfast growing up. My mom and dad used to cook this for me, my younger brother and sister every Saturday morning."

I smiled.

"After breakfast, you need to get ready. We have a field trip today."

'How are we going to get around?"

"I already have it all taken care of."

After getting dressed, Que led me outside to his new car. Waiting outside was a 2016 Subaru Outback. We got into the car and drove away from the hotel.

"Are you sure you want to go back to Scotts-dale?" I asked.

"We can go anywhere we damn well please. Besides, we aren't getting out of the car out here. This is a sightseeing tour."

I nodded my head.

"Just enjoy the ride."

We drove past a small elementary school.

"This is where I went to elementary school, Sonoran Sky."

We drove a few more miles and turned onto 128th Street. Que pointed to the left as we drove towards another school. "This is the middle school that my brother and I went to, Mountainside Middle School." We got onto the 10 freeway and drove for a few miles. We got off and after a few more blocks, we turned onto a street named East Virginia Ave. We stopped right in the front of the school. Que turned and looked at me.

"And this is where I went to high school, where it all changed. Coronado High School."

I was about to ask him what he meant by that, but he turned up the music on his phone and drove off.

"Before you start, I know you want to ask me what I meant by that but I can't give everything away in one night. I will tell you something new every day. Deal?"

I nodded my head. "Deal."

We ate leftover spaghetti for dinner. It tasted better the second time around. I washed the dishes for him and went into the bedroom. I heard the water running in the bathroom and knew that he was nervous and had to calm down. There were places that even I couldn't reach within him and it broke my heart. I changed into my pajamas and waited in the bed for him. I felt that we needed to reconnect. After a few minutes, he turned the water off and opened the door. Turning off the light in the bathroom, he walked towards the bed and laid down next to me. I leaned over and started kissing his neck and reached down towards his cock. Before I was able to grab him, he took my hand and stopped me. He turned around and gave me a kiss on the lips.

"As much as I want you right now, I can't make love to you while you still have Que on the brain. I need you to get to know Evan first, to love Evan first before we do anything else."

Shocked, I jerked my hand back. "You said that how you felt about me was Evan. So what are you talking about?"

"The feelings for you are from Evan, but you love Que. You're gonna get what you've been asking for since the beginning. I just want to make sure that you actually love Evan and not Que."

I got up. "I told you I loved you after people

held me at gunpoint, kidnapped me and threatened to rape me. I still looked to you, and you're telling me that I may not love the real you." I cried, tears spilling down my face. "So it was all not worth it. I need to go back to New York."

Que stared straight ahead, refusing to make eye contact with me. "The ones who mattered the most, the ones who were good, left and they knew the real me. You might be another one."

I felt like he punched me in the stomach. I ran into the living room and laid on the couch, tears burning trails down my face. He didn't bother to come after me. I let the sound of the crickets outside of the patio door lull me to sleep.

I awoke in the morning to find Que sitting in the love seat staring at me. He leaned over to me. "Get dressed."

We drove about an hour south out of the Phoenix. I hadn't really said anything to Que since last night. He also wasn't making too much of an effort to reach out to me either. We got off on Maricopa Drive and saw a sign saying Ak-Chin Indian Reservation. I turned to Que. We pulled in and drove up to the Harrah's Casino.

I uttered my first words to him in a long time. "You really want to gamble?"

He turned to me. "This is the end of the story. This is why I say I made good investments. I'm an investor in this casino and I get a payment every month. Not only because I am an investor, but also because my father was First Nations, Ak-Chin to be exact.

My eyes opened wide. "You're half Native American?"

"Yes, I am." He answered. "I still have family here. I haven't seen them in a long time. My grandma and a couple of uncles and cousins still live here. Before I got caught up with all this shit, I was going to make a trip. I just wanted to make sure the coast was clear. Had to make sure my family was okay. I don't know if I want to introduce them to you just yet because I think you should meet my parents first. My parents are here too. I can take you to see them."

I nodded my head and smiled. "Sure. Let's go."

We pulled out of the Harrah's parking lot and headed down West Farrell Road. In about four minutes we turned on to Indian Route 14, where we came up on a cemetery. My heart instantly sank. We parked and got out of the car. I took his hand as we walked past rows and rows of tombstones until he slowed up and let go of my hand. He walked up to two headstones and dropped to his knees. He hummed and chanted a little before touching each headstone. I began to cry. He stood up and turned to me, grabbing my hand.

"Hey mom, pops. It's me, Evan. I wanted to finally introduce you to someone. Her name is Jazmine. I know you can hear me in the ether, and maybe you brought her to me. But I know if you were still in this world, you'd love her. I do." He turned to me. "My father's name was Robert Red River Miles and my mother's name was Annetta Miles."

I grabbed his arm and wrapped it around me. I rested my head on his shoulder and we just stood there. We drove the whole way home in silence. We went into the suite and I instantly went to the bathroom and turned the water on for him. He smiled as he walked past me. I gave him a kiss on the cheek as he entered the bathroom and closed the door.

I sat down in the living room and curled up into a ball on the couch.

"Jazzy?"

I was about to turn around. "Please don't turn around." Que said.

I nodded my head and faced the TV.

Que continued, "My father died from cancer when I was fourteen years old, or more so should I say, he committed suicide because he was terminal. I had it all as a little boy, my sister, bro and I. We lived in Scottsdale and had family trips. I would go to the res every weekend to visit my grandparents." I heard his voice crack and all I wanted to do was reach out to him.

"The cancer took him quickly. It was pancreatic. He tried to keep us away from him while he died. He intentionally overdosed on drugs and my mom watched and there was nothing we could do. My parents were high school sweethearts. She was disowned by her parents for marrying out of her race. My dad's parents took her on the res and raised her until my parents got married. So my dad was literally all she ever had. Her breakdown happened soon after. She stopped feeding us and taking care of us and we were put in a home about a year after my father died. My sister and brother went to my grandma and she couldn't take me in with me being the oldest. A lot of things happened to me in foster care, but most importantly I was taught to hustle and steal. I would run away from my foster parents to go and visit my mother, but she refused to see me. I guess I looked too much like my dad for her to face me. Shortly after I heard that my mom killed herself. I was fifteen years old. When I was sixteen years old, I was adopted by a loving veterinarian and his wife, but by then I was too far gone."

My face was so wet with tears. I curled up tighter and sobbed silently.

Que continued, voice cracking slightly, "So to keep from putting them through any more pain of constantly bailing me out of juvenile hall, suspensions and the eventual expulsion from Coronado High School, I upped and ran away to Miami. I mean, I was an honor student in all advanced placement classes and my mom couldn't handle me, so how could complete strangers handle me at my worst? I never finished high school. And that is all for tonight." The bedroom door was shut behind me. I heard the sound of running water.

I sat there dumbfounded, almost unable to move because of the pain. I thought back to all of the times I had judged people for the mistakes they made. Most of the time, I didn't know the reasoning behind someone's actions. I grew up in a protected environment. Although I was raised in Chicago, me and my friends and family were far removed from the violence that my city was known for. We only heard about the shootings on the south side of Chicago, and I never personally knew anyone who was affected by the madness. I only somewhat identified because their faces were brown like mine. Hearing Que's story helped me to understand just a little bit how someone could get caught up in the life. Sometimes you gotta to do what you gotta do to survive.

I stood up and completely stripped down. I walked into the bedroom where I could still hear the water running through the bathroom door. I sat on the bed and waited for him. He turned off the water and came out only in a towel. The water was glistening like little diamonds off his body. I stood up and saw his body stand at attention through the towel. I walked over to him and took his hand. I pulled him towards me, stopping just before we reached the bed. I caressed his face and kissed him gently, and then with the tip of my tongue, I licked the drops of water from his chest, down his stomach, and under his navel. I removed the towel from his hips and swirled my tongue until I reached his head and enveloped his whole shaft in my mouth. Working my hands, I sucked and licked up and down his seam. He held my head in place and threw his head back in pleasure. He then pulled himself out of my mouth and held my head, staring into my eyes.

While panting, he said, "As much as I want this, I can't do this."

I looked up at him, "Why not?" I stood up.

Que swallowed hard, "Because I feel like I robbed you of the chance to honestly offer me your body. All the times that we made love before, even that very first night, it was Que you were making love to. Not Evan. I need you to accept Evan in here." Que pointed to my heart. "Before you accept him here." He then put his hand in between my legs and began to gently rub my pearl. I began to moan and grind my hips against his hand. Que pulled me against him and started kissing my neck.

"Whose name do you want to call out? Who is making you feel this way?" he whispered in my ear.

Unable to control myself, I said, "Que!"

Que then stopped and pulled his hands away. "Exactly!" he said.

I stood there, embarrassed. But I loved Evan.

"We'll see if you're still hot for me, after I finish my story. We still have a couple days to go. Good night, Jazmine."

He turned off the lights. I got in bed and he threw his arm around me. Throughout the night, I laid there, wondering how I could reach him. I knew that I could.

I woke up early and took off the necklace and bracelet. I laid them on the nightstand near his phone so they would be the first things he saw when he woke up. I cooked a breakfast of sausage and blueberry pancakes with orange juice and waited. About thirty minutes later, Que emerged from the bedroom and smiled at the layout.

"You took off the necklace and bracelet. Why?"

"Because those were gifts that Que gave me. I hope you like breakfast."

"It smells edible, but we'll see."

"Ha, ha," I said as I sat next to him.

"I heard you college women can't cook."

"Just try my food, mister."

Que took a forkful of pancake and plugged his nose. He then chewed it.

"Pretty good. Beautiful, smart, courageous and can cook. I lucked up."

"You sho did," I said, winking.

I took a few bites of food. "Babe?"

He looked up at me, "Yes?"

"What was the nickname your dad gave you?"

Que was startled and sat his fork down. He smiled at the memory. "My dad used to call me Evan Proud Eagle. He called me that because I was smart."

I smiled at him. "That's amazing."

"We have another field trip today. Be ready by 10."

We drove to a Greyhound station and parked the car. We got out and sat on a stone divider near the parking lot.

"This is where I sat when I bought my one-way ticket to Miami. I had only one duffle bag. It had a few dollars in it, a pair of J's, some clothes and some gummy bears. I wanted to get as far away from Arizona as I possibly could. I saw all the photos of Miami and the women and I was like, oh my God. So I left in the middle of the night and never saw my adopted parents again. It's been about eleven years or so."

I nodded my head. "So with all these field trips we've been taking. Is it safe to say that we're going to Miami soon?"

"You just want me in jail, don't you?"

I moved my hand from side to side, laughing. "Kind of."

He grabbed my hand and held it. "So, once I got to Miami, I alternated between sleeping on the streets and living in youth hostels. I was stealing here and there and I was able to pull off a small robbery at a local jewelry store. While I was at the hostel, I made the mistake of taking out my merch and that's where I met Alisha."

I bristled at her name. Que continued to hold my hand and stare at me. I forced myself to listen.

Que continued, "I thought I was sitting by

myself when I heard her call me out. I turned around and she asked me where I got the jewels from. I said it was my mom's but she didn't believe me and started flirting with me. I was kind of a chubby nigga and a nerd so it was safe to say that women, no matter how they looked, weren't checking for me. So when she was talking to me, being cute, I was hooked. She took my virginity that same night. For a while, she could get me to do anything for her. We had a similar history, so we bonded that way too, and she introduced me to rest of the crew. Once she realized I was smart and good at computers, I eventually became the ringleader. We were our own little family. Although we fucked on and off while we was in the theft ring, she was never my girl. I just couldn't claim her. I wanted someone like my mother; good, sacrificing, wholesome."

I relaxed a little bit. Que stood up.

"Time to go."

We made our way back to the hotel. I was glad to be back inside. Sitting in that 100-degree heat had me feeling some type of way. I sat on the couch as Que turned on the air condition-ing. I fell asleep on the couch.

A couple hours later, I found myself in the

bedroom. Que was laying on the bed, staring straight in the air. I lifted up my head and kissed him on the cheek. He wrapped his arm around me.

"I wanted to be the proud eagle for my father. And for my mother. I always wanted to be a civil engineer and go back and help my people on the reservation. I was really good at computers too, and I was able to break into systems all the time. I remember one time, I hacked the school website and gave everyone A's in all their classes and perfect attendance on MISIS. They still haven't figured out who did it."

I laughed. "That's funny. Can you hack and give me an 800 credit score on Experian?"

He turned and smiled at me. "I'll try."

"That's all I ask."

Que continued, "All in all, I wanted to help people and do good. I kind of thought of myself as a modern day Robin Hood, stealing from the rich and giving to the poor. I targeted my victims that way. My money I either invested or I donated. I had to find a way to make good from a bad situation."

I sat up and caressed his face. "That's all you can do."

"I always wanted a family because mine was destroyed. But I knew I couldn't do that while I was still in the life, so I made my exit as best I could. But the past... well it has a way of catching up to you when you don't tie up the loose ends. And here we are today, in this shit situation. Since day one, I wanted a family with you, a beautiful brown-skinned girl and boy. I want to take care of and protect you and our seeds. I hated lying to you but I wanted to protect you. Not from Evan, but from what Evan had done in his previous life."

My eyes widened. "Really?"

Que turned onto his side and stared directly into my eyes. "Yes. When I saw you, the ancestors whispered to me, that's her."

I blushed.

Que continued, "I've done a lot of bad things in my life, but I've never killed or even hurt anyone. I was talking shit when I said I had women on the corner. Alisha did that shit but I stayed out of it. I would sometimes use Alisha to lure a nigga away from his shit so we could rob him, but that was the most I did. Even though I choose to not have my chest puffed out all the time, doesn't mean I ain't with it. The real move in silence."

I sat up and stared at him. He stared at me back and smiled. "That's all I'm going to tell you. If I go into who I robbed and what I stole, that puts you in a situation where they can use you against me, or put you in jail for not cooperating. I can't have that.

I nodded my head. "I understand."

"So, you finally got your way."

"I always do."

"So the question is, who do you love?"

I swallowed hard and looked down at my hands. This was the moment of truth, where I admit everything. I looked back up at him. "I met a man named Que about six months ago. Right away, I was impressed by his style, his flair, his smoothness.

Que lowered his head and looked at his hands. I leaned over and lifted up his chin, staring into those beautiful golden tiger eyes.

I continued. "As the days turned into months, I got to see this goofy, shy, funny, intelligent man underneath that smooth gorgeous exterior. He knew how to cook, he read books, he was absolutely brilliant. Then seven days ago, I saw a criminal who tried to turn his life around and got caught up again. And yesterday and today, I saw the young kid who had everything and lost it all at such a young age who had to do what he had to do. Some women wait years to learn their man and see growth, but you gave me all of that in less than six months."

Que sat up, still staring at me. I met his gaze and smiled.

"You said your name was Que, but what you gave me was Evan. And I love Evan. Evan was who was on the plane with me, at the Carlyle hotel. Evan was the man who showed me New York and Arizona and who was ready to die to protect me. I love Evan Proud Eagle."

Evan grabbed the back of my head and kissed me with such heat that I thought I would melt. He laid me down on the bed and pulled my shirt over my head. He held it over my face as he kissed down my neck, down the center of my chest, and then traced his lips over to my left breast before swirling his tongue around my nipple. I arched my back and moaned as he then teased my right nipple with his tongue. He then came back up and pulled my shirt off.

"I want you to watch me," he said as he grabbed my left breast again and began to suck my nipple. I grabbed the back of his head. He traced his tongue up my neck and kissed me again. I pulled off his shirt and ran my hands up and down his muscular back. I missed him so much, the warmth of his body, his scent and the way he felt between my legs.

"I love you more than anything. I love every inch of you." He kissed my heart, down my stomach. As he ran his hands up and down my body, he kissed my hips and thighs before finding my pearl. Lifting up my hips, he devoured me.

"I missed this," he said between kisses. I held the back of his head as I climaxed all over him. He kissed his way back up my body and turned me around, pulling me up into the doggy style position. He gave my lower lips another kiss and licked up my back before grabbing my hips and entering me. I threw my head back in pleasure as I felt him part my walls. I missed how he felt, how he filled me up to the brim. He was so gentle as he made love to me. He pulled me up and kissed me while he ran his hands across my breasts and my pearl.

"Fuck. I love you so much," he whispered in my ear.

"I love you too," I said as he brought me to another orgasm.

Evan then laid me flat on my stomach and turned me around. "I want to look at how beautiful you are."

He stared into my eyes taking in a sharp breath as he gently entered me. I felt at home in his embrace. He moved gently in and out of me and my hips moved gently in sync with him. I wrapped my legs around him and threw my head back as I came all over him. He licked up my neck and whispered in my ear.

"Give me my child."

I looked at him and nodded my head. He thrusted deep inside me and grunted, staring into my eyes. I felt him pulsate inside me.

I was his forever.

CHAPTER 5

Tami

I needed something else to think about besides this Jordan foolishness. This nigga was straight up crazy with this shit. It had been about a month or so since Jordan came up to my doorstep with the foolery. One moment he was calling me, crying about how he loved me and then the very next moment he was calling me a stupid fucking bitch. The nigga really needed to make up his mind before I made it up for him. I wanted to talk to Jazzy about it, but I think she's going through her own issues. We used to talk or at least text every day, but now it changed to every couple of days, which was unlike her. I know that when women meet someone they're really into, they tend to put their focus on that person. I've been guilty of it myself, but I wished I knew where she was so that I could visit her. I needed a break from New York and I also needed to see my girl. Chris did everything he could to make me feel secure, but even though he was my man, there were some things that only your girls can help you with. After what happened with Jordan, he didn't need to deal with all this shit.

After what happened, I called my brothers just to put them up on game about Jordan. You had to be a special kind of stupid to try to rile up a chick that had three brothers and a father who played in the NFL. But it takes all types to live in the world. I made them promise not to say anything to our parents. My brothers initially wanted me to put in a transfer from my job and come home to Chicago. I understood where they were coming from but I couldn't give up my life for something as insignificant as Jordan. Ultimately, Mike and Tony said if shit got worse, it was nothing but a word. What I loved about my brothers was how they could get things done and no one would be the wiser.

The last time I spoke to Jazmine was a few days ago. She seemed kind of out of it, rushing me off of the phone. Que must really have been giving her a run for her money. She deserved to be happy. At least one of us was. Things were going great with Chris, but Jordan's last words to me were haunting. Chris didn't take it too lightly either. Although we were on watch, we didn't let it stop us from continuing our romance. Instead of taking our cars out, we would use Lyft or Uber to get around. We would end our nights making love. But the stress of avoiding phone calls and texts were still getting on my nerves.

Then one day it all took its toll.

"Focus Tamera," I said to myself. "You can't let nothing get in the way of your money." I looked at the computer screen and tried to make sense of the numbers. I had to be on my "A" game with this. Darthon Publishing was one of my biggest clients and I had to make sure that the figures all matched. My phone started vibrating. I looked down at the caller ID. It was Jordan again. Literally ten times today. I rolled my eyes and started running the numbers again. My phone vibrated again indicating that Jordan left a message. The only reason why I listened to that dumb ass's messages was because I wanted to make sure I had evidence in case he threatened to do something to me or what not. I may need it in case I had to cry self-defense.

I pressed play and put the phone to my ear.

"Tami!" Jordan whimpered. "Why won't you speak to me? Why are you doing this to me? You are such a selfish fucking bitch for not talking to me. You putting that stupid nigga over what we had. Three fucking years, Tamera. Was you fucking him while you were with me? I knew your pussy would feel funny sometimes." He paused, "I didn't mean that. I'm sorry. I'm just mad, mad that I can't talk to you or hold you. I've been watching you, Tami. You ain't gonna always have that nigga around you. I will make you mine again."

The voice messaged ended. I shook my head in disgust. That tore it. I needed to go home for the rest of the day. I emailed my boss to ask him if I could work from home. Moments later, I got a response saying yes. I then emailed Chris to let him know I was leaving. As I was packing up my purse and preparing to leave, I received a text from Chris.

"I'm going to the Chicago office for a couple of days. I think I need you to come with me. Go home and pack your bags. I'll meet you in two hours."

I smiled and replied, *"Bet."*

I left the office and took a Lyft home instead of the subway. I was afraid of possibly being caught off guard by Jordan. I got home in about 15 minutes, which was very good for Manhattan traffic in the middle of the day. On the ride home, I had already planned out about seven outfits that I would put together to see my family and friends. I thought I would stay an extra three days to catch up with my folks. I wondered if it was also time for the family to meet Chris. We have been together for about six months and, I already got to know his people. It was about time to return the favor. I've only brought Jordan to meet the family, and it took a year for that to happen. Chris would be the first one to meet them on their home turf. I entered the house and dropped my purse on the table. I ran upstairs and took out my Louis Vuitton luggage. Chicago was gorgeous in the spring to summer transition. It would be amazing eighty-degree weather. I packed a mix of dresses, skinny jeans and off-white t-shirts. Perfect for days in and nights out. After picking out the perfect shoes and jewelry, I was all ready to go.

I called Chris, "I'm all ready. I hope you are too. You just might find yourself lucky enough to meet my parents."

Chris replied back, "It's about damn time. I'll be there in a few."

"I can go on without you. Do you want me to just call an Uber? Let me know which airline and I'll meet you at the gate."

"No babe, I want to ride with you. You know why. Anyway, I got our tickets, first class. Let's enjoy our first official trip as a couple."

"Bet." I hung up the phone.

I picked up my one travel case and went downstairs. Being a child of the world, with attending boarding schools and spending months abroad, I was an expert packer. I was usually able to fit at least a week's worth of outfits and shoes in one medium-sized suitcase. While I waited, I decided to treat myself with a glass of wine. I loved Stella Rosa and other fruity wines

Since the thirty minutes that I was home and packing, Jordan called my phone about four more times. No messages left. Thank God. I didn't need another headache. As I sat there, I contemplated how my parents and brothers would receive Chris. My mom's biological clock was ticking for me. Having a Trini mother, I knew the first thing coming out of her mouth would be when are we marrying and having some grandbabies. I needed to plan the perfect exit strategy for when that conversation would come up. Otherwise, I thought they would get along wonderfully. However, I wasn't going to introduce him to my girls right away. Some things are best kept a secret. Besides, he already met Jazmine and that was all he needed to know right now.

I picked up the phone and dialed Jazzy. After a few rings, she answered the phone.

"Hello?" Jazzy said.

"Hey booski. So the dead has arisen?"

'Girl, you ain't never lied."

"How's it going with Que?"

There was a little bit of hesitation in her voice. I was waiting for her answer.

"Everything is going great." She eventually replied.

I rolled my eyes. She was straight up lying.

"So, let's cut to the chase. Where are you, Jazzy and when are you coming back to New York?"

There was silence on the other line. "I've been in Arizona and I don't know when I'm coming back to New York. It may be in a couple of weeks or it may be in a couple months."

I sat up straight. "Arizona?" I asked.

"Yes. He's taken me on a U.S. tour, which included Puerto Rico. I've always wanted to go to Arizona to see the Painted Desert. You know that. Well he took me there as a surprise. It's absolutely beautiful."

I nodded my head. "I'm happy for you."

"How're you and Chris?"

"We're good. Great actually."

"You still having problems with Jordan?" she asked

"The nigga crazy. I be trying to tell these boys about the Trini nani. It's only for grown men, but that was my fault for messing with him."

Jazzy laughed. "But you redeemed yourself by getting a real one, too."

I heard my message alert and looked down at the phone. Chris had texted that he was going to be there in a few minutes. I put the phone back to my ear.

"I sure do, girl. That was just him. I'm, well I should say we, are going home for a few days. I'm going to introduce him to the family."

Jazzy squealed. "Oh my God, that is a huge step. I wish I could go back home, just to see how that would go."

"You should meet me there." I replied.

"I wish I could. But send my love to everyone." Jazzy said.

"I know." I heard a knock. I stood up and began to walk towards the door. "I'll talk to you later my love. Chris is here. I'll tell the family you said hello."

I hung up the phone and opened the door, expecting Chris. However, I was staring at the barrel of a twenty-two. I moved away and tried to push the door closed but Jordan pushed his way inside and slammed the door shut. I ran upstairs while texting Chris to let him know that Jordan had gotten in my house. Just as I pressed send, Jordan grabbed me from behind. My phone flew out of my hands. He bear-hugged me and threw me on the couch. Jordan pointed the gun at me and sat down in the chair across from me. He looked to my left at my suitcase.

"Going somewhere?" He asked.

I tried to maintain my composure even though every fiber of my being wanted to sink my nails into his eyes. I just didn't want him to shoot me. He had the same crazy look in his eyes that he had the last time he was at my house. I watched him closely. I crossed my legs and smiled at him.

"Yes. I was going to go home for a few days. A family member is sick." I said as calmly as I could.

"Are they okay?" he asked.

"I'll find out when I get there. You know how my family is." I replied.

Jordan set the gun down on his lap, with the barrel pointing at me. "Tami, I don't have the gun to hurt you. I don't want to do anything to you but love you. I just needed it because I knew I couldn't get in the house any other way to talk to you. I watched you leave by yourself from your office and I watched you come home also, so I knew he wasn't here."

"He doesn't go everywhere I go." I replied.

"Is he going with you to Chicago?" Jordan asked.

"No."

Jordan nodded his head. "We now have this time to talk. I've really missed you." I watched him caress the gun. He looked back up at me. I smiled as best I could.

"I miss you too. I've been waiting to talk to you. It's just with Chris, it's…"

Jordan leaned over and caressed my face. "I know. I know that's not like you." He interrupted. "You always been my Trini fire, but you're loyal. And that's one of the many reasons why I fell in love with you."

Swallowing hard, I nodded my head. "It's good to know I'm appreciated. That's what made you so special to me."

I heard my phone ring. I turned my head towards the stairs.

"Go get your phone, baby." Jordan said.

I nodded my head and got up. I was searching for the phone, which I eventually found on one of my steps. Chris called. I continued to feel around acting as if I had to find the phone, typing to Chris, that Jordan had a gun and was in my house. I didn't wait for his response when I picked up the phone. I turned around to find Jordan standing behind me pointing the gun at my stomach. I closed my eyes waiting for the trigger to be pulled.

"Who was that on the phone?" Jordan whispered gently.

I refused to answer. Jordan extended his palm towards me.

"Give it to me." he asked.

I handed him the phone. I prayed that Chris wouldn't respond to the text I just sent. He looked at my missed calls. Handing me the phone, he said, "Chris. Humph. Call him and let him know I'm here."

I dialed his number and put the phone to my ear. "Hello, Chris. Jordan is here. We can't do this anymore. I don't care because Jordan is here and that's all I'm going to say. Okay. Bye."

I hung up the phone and sat in on the table.

Jordan pulled me towards and gave me a kiss. My arms were in front of my chest as he wrapped his arms around me. He still had that weird, sour smell. I tried to push him away, but he still had the gun and I didn't want him to pull the trigger on me. I had to be smart about this. So I did my best to succumb to him, but I wanted to throw up in his mouth. "So good to know you're mine again." He started kissing my neck and putting his hand up my skirt. He pulled open my shirt and popped my right breast out of my bra cup. Looking at my pierced nipple, he said, "Mmm, one of the other things I missed about you." He flicked my nipple ring with his tongue. "Tastes like cherries, just like I remember it."

Dropping down to his knees, he moved my thong aside and began sucking on my clit. I couldn't believe this was happening. I was about to be raped in my own home and there was no one there to help me.

"Do you miss this baby?" he murmured.

Vomit in my throat, I responded "Yes, I do. But before we do this, there are other things we have to talk about first."

He stopped and looked up at me. "Like what?"

I nodded my head and smiled, holding back tears. "Shall we sit down first?"

We walked back to the couch. He sat next to me, removing the gun from his waistband and holding it. He then reached for me again, but I put my hands up. "Hard to get. You always knew your worth. So what do you need me to do to fully win you back?" Jordan asked.

"I want to take this to the next level. We've been together for almost three years and it's time that we talk about settling down and starting a family."

"I wanted to marry you."

I nodded. There was a knock on the door.

"I think that's the Uber driver ready to take me to the airport."

"I'll go with you!" Jordan exclaimed.

"You need to pack."

"I can buy something there," Jordan replied.

"Jordan, please. This is not the time." I said

The knocking became more frantic.

"Come on, babe. They always call. Uber doesn't knock, Tami."

I heard Chris scream my name through the door. He was knocking and kicking the door. I saw Jordan point the gun at the door.

Tears flowed down my face. I had to save Chris. I turned to Jordan, "Baby, please don't shoot him. I don't want you to go to jail. I need you here with me. Please!" I cried.

Jordan turned towards me and wiped the

tears from my face. It took all I could not to slap his hands away from me.

"Shh, baby. We have this. Now go to the door and open it. That's all you have to do." Jordan pushed the barrel of the gun into my side. I found myself moving forward.

"I'll tell you when to open the door, my love." Jordan whispered in my ear as we walked towards the door. We stopped and my hand touched the door knob. I looked up at him.

Chris continued to knock frantically and then stopped. Jordan then looked at me and nodded towards the door.

"Open the door, baby," he whispered.

I bit my lower lip and flung open the door. I locked eyes with Chris and he nodded his head slightly. I moved out of the way. He barged in and turned around. Out of the corner of my eye, I saw Jordan aim the gun at Chris. Chris turned around, reaching behind his back.

"Chris!" I screamed as I heard the loud bang of the gunshot. My ears began to ring and then it was darkness.

CHAPTER 6

Jazmine

I hadn't heard from Tami for a couple of days. I wanted to hear all about the Chicago trip and how Chris and her family got along. Her brothers were hard on any man that even sniffed near Tami, but Mr. Marsden, or pops as I always called him, was truly next level. Although, they would mess with Chris, I knew everything would be good between them. Chris seemed like a decent man that really cared about Tami. That's what meant the most to me. But I still wanted to hear it from her. By now, she would've had me on FaceTime with all of the girls. Maybe she was having too much fun.

Someone needed to. Because of circumstances, I kind of preferred to be by myself for the time being. I didn't want to risk telling her anything. I didn't want to tell anyone anything. No matter what the verdict was, I wanted to put this nasty situation behind me and move on. Plus, knowing she was gonna talk all kinds of shit, coupled with possibly losing Evan was the last thing I needed to deal with. I knew she would reach out to me eventually.

I did my best to make the most of our time together. We kept a low profile because we didn't want to attract any more attention to ourselves. The press got a hold of the story and had already found the mugshot of Evan. Before they could find out where we stayed or be recognized by the staff, we left in the middle of the night, with only the clothes on our back. Evan took me to Harrah's. In order to make himself look a little different, he started to grow out his hair. We stayed holed up in the hotel. Due to being on Indian land, the news media was not allowed on the land unless they had consent. Needless to say, it wasn't given. So we knew we were safe. We lived off of sunlight and sex. Every day until the trial, we made love as if he was going off to war. And he was. We didn't know what would happen during the trial and we wanted our last memories together to be of love and happiness. One night, as we laid next to each other in bed, he was absentmindedly caressing my stomach.

"What would happen if I became pregnant?" I asked.

"I'd be complete," he said and kissed me on my temple.

"Even if they find you guilty?" I asked.

Evan was silent for a moment. I turned around and laid my head on his shoulder. He kissed my forehead. The next day Evan was on the phone with his lawyers. Over the next couple days, Evan left the hotel each morning for face to face meetings with his team. When he returned, I would try to pry information out of him. The only thing he would say to me was, "I'm doing what I need to do to make sure you're safe. And that whatever the outcome of the trial is, it will have the least effect on me."

The night before the trial, Evan went outside on the patio and stared at the night sky. I heard him humming as I walked to the door.

"Baby, time to go to bed," I said as I kissed him on the back of his neck.

"I'll be inside in a few minutes. I'm talking to my mom and dad right now."

I nodded my head and stepped back into the house. On the day of the trial, he dressed in his Sunday finest, an immaculately tailored navy blue suit and cream silk shirt. I knotted his sky blue tie and gave him a kiss on the lips. Hand in hand, during the whole ride, we took an Uber to the courthouse where the press was waiting. Evan turned to me and kissed me on the lips.

"I want you to stay home until they're prepared to reach the verdict. I don't want anyone knowing your face or your name, anything."

"Please let me stay with you." I pleaded.

Evan interrupted me. "I do want you there too, but I just can't risk it. Please respect what I'm saying to you. I want you on the res and safe. In fact, since they don't know what you look like, go back to the Royal Palms and pack up our stuff. I'll have someone deliver whatever you can't bring with you by hand."

"But I...," I said.

He pressed his finger to my lips, silencing

me. "My trial is apart from the others. You don't have to worry about that, but I want us to be separate until we hear a verdict. I'll be able to contact you." He kissed me again and opened the car door. Evan was immediately swarmed by reporters. The tears fell from my eyes.

I reached the Royal Palms about an hour later and began to pack. We were separated once again. I sprayed the bed pillows with my favorite scent to remind him of me. As I carried my bags to the front door, I looked around at the suite one more time. At the dining room where we had dinner, at the bed where we made love, at the aptly named love seat where we, well I, finally admitted my feelings for him. I turned off the lights and walked out to my Uber driver.

About an hour and a half later, I was alone again in my room at the Harrah's. I put down my bags and laid out on the bed. I knew they wouldn't televise this trial, so I had my phone set to alert me on any new developments for the story. I had to keep my mind occupied until four o'clock when court would adjourn for the day. I picked up my computer and began to work. I still had a few projects to work on from my Phoenix clients. Before I knew it, it was five and my phone alert went off. I picked up my phone and loaded up the app.

"The opening statements from the prosecution and defense for the trial of the people against Evan Miles began today. Last month, a Miami theft ring in which Miles was the former ringleader attempted to rob a series of jewelry stores at the Scottsdale Fashion Square. The prosecution as well as other members of the theft ring have alluded to Miles as being the mastermind behind the attempted robbery. The defense for Miles have stated that their defendant was not found at the scene and thus has no involvement in the case. News Five will keep you posted with any additional developments."

I sighed and turned off my computer. I got a text on my phone. It simply read.

"I love you. We got this."

I replied back. *"I know. I love you too."*

I laid down and tried to go to sleep.

I thought the trial would only last for a few days. All the others did and they were given swift sentences ranging from ten to fifteen years. Over the past two weeks, I read about a new verdict for each member of the Miami Ten, as the press had named them. For Streetz's trial, Evan submitted a written statement detailing how Streetz, real name Michael Sanders, was completely innocent. His lawyers, which were paid for by Evan, ran their case on Streetz being forced to partake in the robbery because of threats made against his family. However, the jury still found him guilty and gave him a year-long sentence. After reading this latest verdict, I became even more afraid for my Evan Proud Eagle.

I read each and every update of the story about Evan. Each day the defense presented new evidence that would exonerate Evan from the robbery. The press also started to dive into his background and financial resources. They mentioned his family and his various invest-ments, all of which were purchased with clean money. Evan was telling me the truth. The trial stretched on for three weeks and all I did during that time was sleep and work. To keep myself from fretting, I found new clients to work for, but with them, I chose to work remotely. They agreed to Skype me for meetings. I was unable to eat, but I had to force myself. The Grub Hub delivery people began to know me by first name and order.

What kept hope alive in me was Evan's texts. Each day, he would find a different way to declare his love for me. I never knew one single sentence could mean so much. While working on a project a month after Evan's trial began, my phone rang. I looked down at the caller ID. It was him. I picked up the phone.

"Hello?"

"My God, it feels good to hear your voice. I miss you so much," Evan sighed.

I held back tears. "Baby, I miss you too."

"I know you've been following the story. I just wanted to let you know before you read it that they will be reaching a verdict tomorrow. Whatever the outcome, I want you there. I want your face to be the last thing I see."

I nodded. "Okay. I'm at Harrah's, still in the same room. What time will you be here?" I said, my throat clogged with emotion.

"I will be there by six," he replied.

"I can't wait to see you."

"Me neither."

"I love you."

"I love you too."

I hung up the phone and laid my head down on the pillow.

Hours later, my phone alerted me to an update to the story. I looked down and read it.

Sure enough, the news report read that all the evidence was heard and each side gave their closing arguments. Jury was called for deliberation. Tomorrow they were going to have a verdict and sentencing. My heart dropped. It was D-Day. Evan arrived around six. When I opened up the door, he was dressed in a hoodie and jeans, holding only one small duffle bag. We just stood and stared at each other for a moment, soaking in each other's presence. Dropping his bag, he walked in and grabbed me, picking me up. I wrapped my legs around him and we fell on the bed. I rolled on top of him. My tears soaked his shirt as I rested my head on his shoulder. He ran his fingers through my hair.

"I missed you too."

"Can I just lay here with you? No words. I just want to listen to your heart beat."

"That's exactly what I had in mind," he whispered and kissed my forehead.

We laid like that for hours. We finally rose up about nine at night, and ordered room service and ate in silence.

"What do you think the verdict will be?"

"It should be not guilty but you know how

that goes," he replied while pointing at the back of his hand. I nodded my head and stood up.

I went over to the bathroom and turned on the shower. When the water was hot enough, I walked back into the bedroom and took Evan's hand.

"Let me cater to you," I whispered to him. I slowly undressed him. I took off my clothes and pulled him into the shower. I ran my hands up and down his body, massaging his tense muscles. Using the bath lily hand soap, I did my best to rub the knots out of his body as I lathered him up. He leaned against the front of the shower as he rinsed off. Kissing his back and shoulders, I reached over and began to stroke his manhood. He threw his head back and let out a groan. I turned him around and kissed his lips while still massaging him. My lips made a trail from his neck and down his chest until I swirled my tongue around his head. He pulled my hair as he began to thrust into my mouth. He pulled himself out of my mouth and lifted me up, leading me out of the shower.

Evan threw me over his shoulder and tossed me onto the bed. He pulled me towards him and laid on top of me, then held my hands above my head and kissed me. The tip of his tongue flicked one nipple and then the other before he pulled me up by my hips and started kissing my lower lips. I opened my legs wide as he quickly brought me to climax. I ground my hips against his face as he licked and inserted one of his fingers inside of me.

Evan licked his fingers as he finished. He then pushed my hips down as he slowly entered me, putting his full weight on me as he penetrated me. Once, he was completely inside of me, he turned his head and stared at me. Every inch of my body was covered and filled with him. He grabbed the back of my hair again and only moved his hips in quick, short strokes that set my body on fire. I wrapped my arms and legs around him and moaned as the pressure built up inside of me. Through heavy breathing, he moaned to me, "I missed hearing my favorite song."

He moved his hips quicker as I began to rake my hands up and down his back. I could barely contain myself, getting louder as he brought me closer to climax. He then lifted himself up and began to barrel down on me. I threw my hips up in response as the last stroke brought me over the edge of ecstasy. I sank my nails into his back as he sucked my left nipple. I left my mark on his back as the waves continued to crash over me. As I began to recover, Evan took his right hand and placed it at the top of my hair. Holding my head down, he thrusted deeper inside of me until he threw his head back and let out a long groan. His muscles tensed as I felt him shudder and release inside of me. He collapsed on top of me and kissed me on the forehead.

"I love you."

"I love you too." I whispered back.

We fell asleep joined together, in each other's embrace.

The routine of the morning after was the same as the first day of Evan's trial. We got ready in silence. I helped him knot his tie and he kissed me on the forehead. We took an Uber to the courthouse. As we pulled up, Evan turned to me.

"I'm going to go in first. I want you to wait until I am inside and the media has moved away from the front of the courthouse before you come in." Evan leaned over to the Uber driver.

"Is it okay if she sits in here for a few extra minutes? I'll give you extra on the side."

The Uber driver nodded his head. Evan took out a twenty-dollar bill and handed it to me.

"I'll see you soon." He kissed me on the forehead and got out of the car. He was immediately surrounded by reporters, but ignored them as he walked up to his lawyer and entered the courthouse. The Uber driver moved down a half a block and we waited. We sat for what seemed like forever, but eventually the crowd of reporters began to dissipate and it was safe for me to go outside. I thanked the driver and handed him the twenty. I walked up the steps of the courthouse and looked at the bulletin in the lobby.

"Room 344, the People versus Evan Miles," I said to myself. I walked over to the elevators and pressed the up button. Today was the day that our lives could change forever. The elevator arrived and I stepped in, pressing the third floor button. The ride seemed to take longer than usual. I exited the elevator and made a left. I opened the door to the courtroom and found a seat near the back. I saw Evan, his shoulders hunched as he sat next to his lawyers. I looked around and out of the corner of my eye, I saw a woman and man, who looked very similar to Evan sitting not too far behind him. Those might have been his brother or sister. I was so happy to know that he hadn't been going through the trial alone. The judge turned towards the jury.

"Will the jury foreperson please stand?" The judge asked. An older white man stood up. I had made it just in time.

"Has the jury reached a unanimous verdict?" the judge continued.

"Yes," the man answered and took out a piece of paper.

I watched as the court clerk stood up and walked over to the foreman. The foreman handed her the piece of paper. She then walked it over and handed it to the judge. He read it in silence and then handed it back to the clerk.

"The jury finds the defendant not guilty."

Thanking God, I smiled and clapped my hands together. Evan straightened up and threw his hands in the air. His lawyers patted him on the back as he shook their hands. Evan stood up and hugged the man and the woman who were sitting behind him.

"The jury is thanked and excused. Court is adjourned," the judge said, and went into the back room. I fought back tears of joy as I stared at Evan. We can start our life anew, free from all of the BS. We could go anywhere. I wanted to head back to New York as soon as possible. I couldn't wait to see what was in store for us. I could tell Evan was looking for me. I walked up to him and he swept me up in his embrace, kissing me. Wrapping his arm around me, he led me over to the man and woman who sat behind him.

"This is Jazmine; the woman I've been telling you about. Jazmine, this is my sister Ariana and my brother, Daniel."

We shook hands. "So this is the woman that's been keeping my brother out of trouble. It's good to see he has something good in his life for a change." Ariana said.

I smiled.

"We hope to see you around more often."

Evan hugged me and kissed me on the forehead. "You will."

"We're going back home to let the family

know that everything is good. Grandma would be happy to see you," Aaron responded. "Please come over after everything is settled. Nice to meet you, Jazmine."

I smiled. "Likewise."

Ariana and Aaron left the courtroom. Evan turned to me. "So, I'm free to go. I'm all yours. For good. If you'll have me."

"Forever is not long enough." We walked out of the courtroom hand in hand.

"So that's your brother and sister? They're beautiful."

Evan laughed. "They all right."

"How did you find them?"

"My brother found me when he heard about the trial. Over the years, we stayed in some kind of contact. Despite everything, there was never any bad blood between us."

"So why didn't you want me to sit here with you during your trial?"

"Because I didn't want to put you through any more unnecessary pain. You've been through too much because of me. For every thing that has happened to you because of me, I will make it up to you. I will spend the rest of my lifetime making it up to you."

"I'll hold you to that," I replied.

I took out my cell phone and ordered an Uber. Evan gave me another kiss. We took the stairs to the first floor, and he looked at me as we approached the exit of the courthouse.

"You ready for this?"

I took my sunglasses out of my purse and put them on. I tied my hair up into a ponytail. "Have we met?" I said.

He smiled as he grabbed my hand and we exited the courthouse. We were immediately surrounded by media. They shoved microphones in his face and began barraging him with questions. I covered my face and turned my head away from the cameras.

"How does it feel to be a free man?"

"Mr. Miles. How do you think the others feel about this outcome? They…"

"Why do you think the jury…"

Evan ignored them and grabbed my hand tightly, leading me through the throng of reporters. This definitely must have been one of the more exciting events to happen in the city in a long time. Out of the corner of my eye, I saw a woman standing at the bottom of the stairs. She was staring at Evan. She looked vaguely familiar to me. I just chalked it up to being another reporter who wanted to catch Evan before he left. I looked at my phone and saw that the Uber drive was only two minutes away from our location. Two more minutes until freedom…

CHAPTER 7

The reporters' voices began to meld together into a mind-numbing drone. I was unable to continue to decipher the questions they were asking Evan. We continued to ignore them. As we walked past the woman standing on the last step, I looked up from my phone to hear a familiar voice. A voice that I never though I would hear again. How did she…

"How does it feel to get away with it?" the woman asked, holding a fake tape recorder up to his lips.

Evan looked up in surprise. It was Alisha. She had on the same black wig she wore at the grocery store. He tried his best to ignore her. She stepped in front of him, blocking our path.

"How does it feel to get away with abandoning your group and leaving me out in the cold?" she asked again.

Evan's jaw tightened and he shook his head. He stood in front of me and moved to the right to walk around her.

"You're lucky I don't say anything right now about you. They are looking for you." Evan said through clenched teeth.

"Are you sure about that?" she said condescendingly.

"How the fuck did you get out? They said they arrested everyone," Evan asked.

"To be so smart, you must've forgotten how to count. There were twelve of us, including you and her."

Evan moved to the right to get around her. I saw our Uber driver pull up to the curb. Just ten more feet until freedom. We could make it. Just a few more steps.

"You're not going to ignore us, Evan. You're not going to ignore me. The courts may have let you go. They may have found you innocent of any wrongdoing, but I won't. You deliberately set us up, and you have to pay!" she screamed as she reached behind her and pulled out a gun. She pointed the gun at me, but Evan quickly pulled me behind him as she pulled the trigger. She shot him once in the chest and in the thigh. I screamed as I felt his blood splatter on me and watched him fall to the ground. I looked around as people screamed and hit the ground.

The sounds of running footsteps and reporters' voices created a cacophony that made my ears bleed. I couldn't think. I dropped to my knees and grabbed Evan's hand. I fumbled for my phone as I dialed 911. I looked up as Alisha pointed the gun at my head. I closed my eyes. Just as she was about to pull the trigger, she was tackled by two court officers. They held her down and handcuffed her.

The reporters tried to surround us to ask me questions, but the court officers created a barrier between us. I was finally able to focus as the phone connected to the operator.

"Hello, 9-1-1 operator, is this an emergency?" The operator said on the other line.

"Yes, a man was shot at the Phoenix courthouse. He was shot on the steps in his chest and thigh. He's bleeding badly. Please come quick-ly!" I screamed.

Evan groaned and writhed in pain. He began to shake. I took his head and laid it in my lap. I felt the cameras on us.

"What is your location again?" The 9-1-1 operator asked.

"Phoenix courthouse. Please hurry."

"We have dispatched paramedics to your location," she replied.

"Thank you." I dropped my phone on the ground. I kissed him on the forehead.

"Baby, I love you so much." I whispered to him.

The Uber driver had called my phone three times, but I didn't answer. I saw him, our future, drive off. All of a sudden, Evan stopped shaking and his hand relaxed a little in mine. I heard his breathing become more shallow. One of the court officers ran up to us and checked on him.

"Baby, please! Hold on baby! Please!" I screamed.

I looked around me, waiting for the ambulance.

"Where are the fucking paramedics?" I screamed.

I looked to the left and heard sirens in the distance.

FIND out what happens next in Loving The Wrong Man Book 4! Available Now!

FOLLOW Mia Black on Instagram for more updates: @authormiablack

LOVING THE WRONG MAN 4

After all they been through, Jazmine and Evan are now faced with a life altering event, that could end their budding romance forever.

Find out what happens in the final installment of Loving The Wrong Man!

Follow Mia Black on Instagram for more updates: @authormiablack

CPSIA information can be obtained
at www.ICGtesting.com
Printed in the USA
LVHW081302260919
632360LV00014B/491/P

9 781072 199923